Franklin and the Thunderstorm

For my neighbor, Amanda — PB

For my mother, who still worries
about thunderstorms — BC

Franklin

FRANKLIN and the FRANKLIN characters are trademarks of Kids Can Press Ltd.

ISBN 0-590-02635-6

Text copyright © 1998 by Contextx
Illustrations copyright © 1998 by Brenda Clark Illustrator Inc.
Interior illustrations prepared with the assistance of Shelley Southern and
Muriel Hughes Wood.
All rights reserved. Published by Scholastic Inc., 555 Broadway, New York, NY
10012, by arrangement with Kids Can Press Ltd. SCHOLASTIC and associated
logos are trademarks and/or registered trademarks of Scholastic Inc.

24 23 22 21 20 19 18 17 16 15   2 3/0

Printed in the U.S.A.   23

First Scholastic printing, March 1998

Franklin and the Thunderstorm

Written by Paulette Bourgeois
Illustrated by Brenda Clark

SCHOLASTIC INC.

New York   Toronto   London   Auckland   Sydney

Franklin could count by twos and tie his shoes. He could name the months of the year and all the seasons. He could read the thermometer, and he checked the barometer every day. Franklin worried about the weather because he was afraid of storms.

One day, Franklin was supposed to play at Fox's house, but the sky was getting dark and the clouds were thick.

"Maybe I shouldn't go," Franklin said to his mother.

She looked out the window. "It probably won't rain until later," she said. "You have time to get to Fox's."

Franklin put on his boots and took the umbrella.

As Franklin hurried to Fox's house, he kept
looking at the sky. The clouds moved quickly,
and wind swirled dirt in the air.
Franklin felt all jumpy inside.

Fox was playing outside when Franklin arrived.

Franklin pointed nervously to the sky. "I think we should go inside, don't you?" he asked.

"Not yet." Fox grinned. "I love watching the clouds move and feeling the wind blow. It's exciting!"

"I think it's scary," said Franklin.

Beaver, Snail, and Hawk came over to play, too.
"My fur feels funny when it's about to storm,"
said Fox.
"My feathers get all ruffled," said Hawk.
Beaver sniffed. "I can smell a storm coming."

The wind became stronger.

Hawk flew loop-the-loops. "Whee!" he cried.

Franklin held on to his hat and shivered.

It was almost as dark as night when big fat raindrops began to fall.

"We should go in!" shouted Franklin.

"No," said Fox. "Follow me."

They raced to the tree house, where it was dry.

"Fox!" called his mother. "Time for everyone to come in."

"It's all right," Fox shouted back. "We're in the tree."

Fox's mother was there in a second. "It's dangerous to be near a tree during a storm," she said. "Lightning strikes tall things first, and you might get hurt."

Franklin held on to Fox's mother all the way from the tree to the house. They were barely in the door when there was a flash of zigzag light.

"Lightning!" shrieked Franklin. He trembled.

KA-BOOM!

"Thunder!" he screamed.

"It's okay, Franklin," said his friends. "We're safe here."

But Franklin had crawled deep inside his shell.

Fox's mother brought treats. Still, Franklin wouldn't come out.

Franklin's friends begged him to play. But Franklin stayed put.

Then, with a flash and a crash, the lights went out.

"Don't worry," said Fox's mother. She lit candles and turned on a flashlight.

"Won't you come out now?" she asked Franklin.

"No thank you," he mumbled.

"Don't be afraid," said Hawk.
"All that noise is just cloud giants
playing drums in the sky."

Franklin peeked out. "Really?"
he asked.

"No it's not," giggled Snail.
"That noise is made when the
giants go bowling."

Franklin came out of his shell.
"But what about the lightning?"

"That's easy," said Hawk. "The
cloud giants are turning their lights
on and off."

Fox smiled. "I think it's the giants
swinging from their chandeliers."

Franklin laughed.

"Giants! That's ridiculous," said Beaver. "Mr. Owl says lightning is a big spark of electricity that travels from the sky to the ground. The spark is so hot that it makes the air around it POP! That's the sound of thunder."

"Amazing!" said Franklin.

Franklin felt a little better. He even played flashlight
tag with his friends.

Soon, there was hardly any lightning. The thunder
was a low rumble from far away, and the rain stopped.

Then the lights went on.

"Storm's over!" said Fox. "Let's go outside and play."

"Look," said Franklin. "A rainbow!"

"I know why the storm is over," Franklin said.
"Those giants heard there's a pot of gold at the
end of every rainbow, and they've gone to find it."
Even Beaver had to smile.